TRIANGLE

by

Mac Barnett

&

Jon Klassen

CANDLEWICK PRESS

This is Triangle.

This is Triangle's house.

This is Triangle in his house.

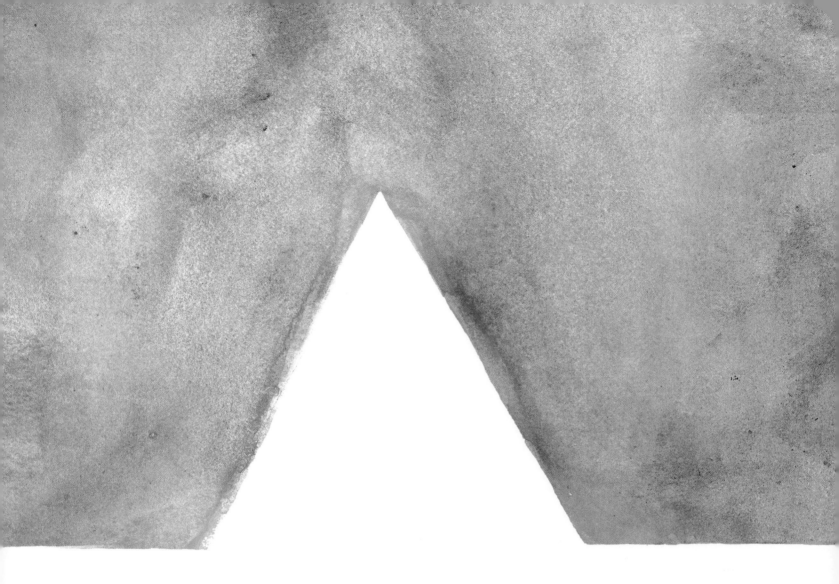

And that is Triangle's door.

One day Triangle walked out his door
and away from his house.

He was going to play a sneaky trick on Square.

He walked past small triangles

and medium triangles and big triangles.

He walked past shapes

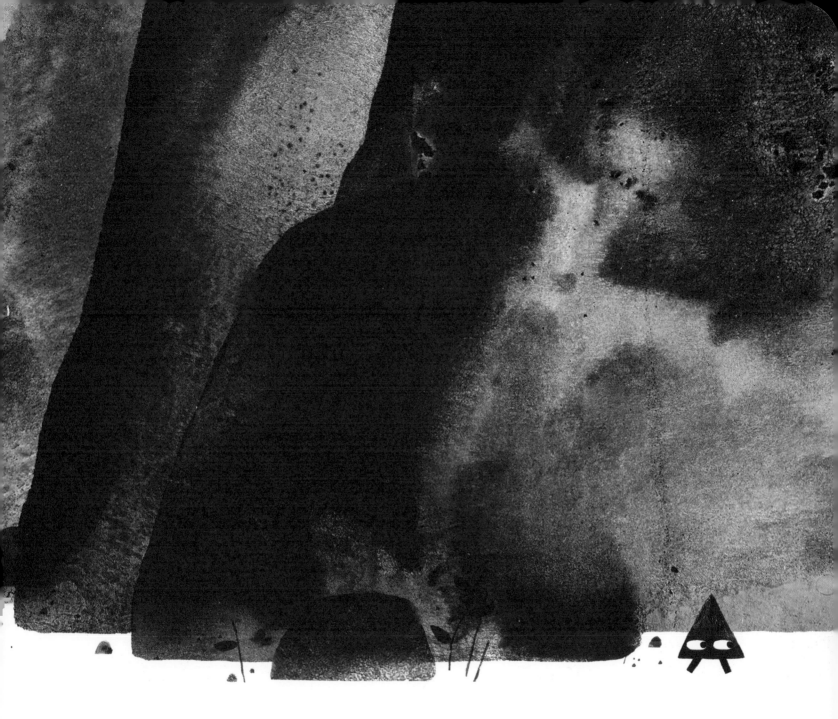

that weren't triangles anymore.

They were shapes

with no names.

He walked until he got to a place

where there were squares.

Still thinking of his sneaky trick,
he walked past big squares

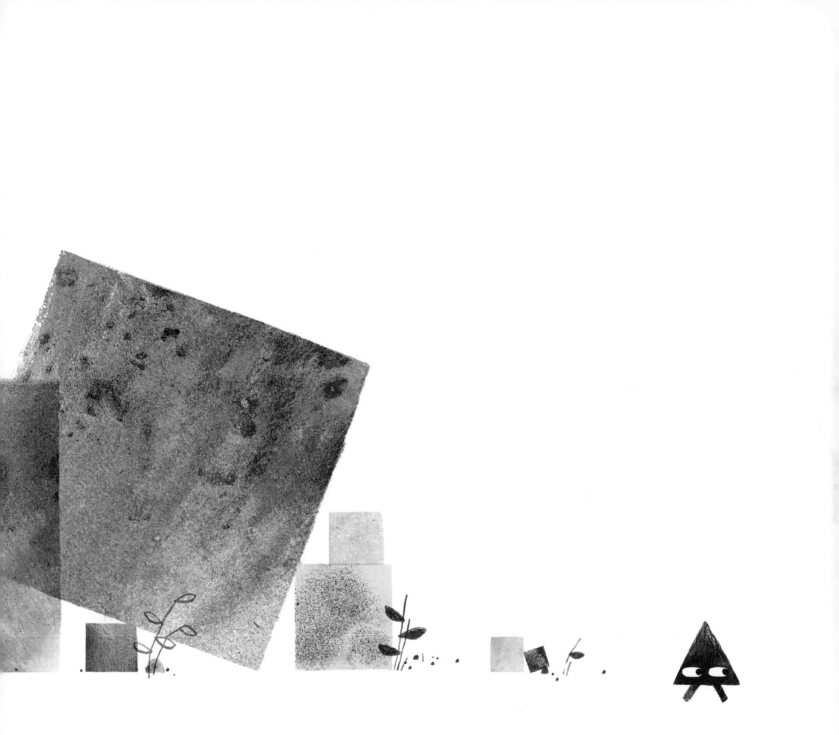

and medium squares and small squares

until he got to Square's house.
"Now," said Triangle,

"I will play my sneaky trick."

Triangle walked up to Square's door

and said "HISS!" just like a snake.

Square was afraid of snakes.

"Oh me oh my!" said Square.

"Go away, you snake! Leave my door!"

"HISS!" said Triangle. "HISS! HISS! HISS!"

"Oh dear dear dear!" said Square.

"How many snakes are out there? Ten?
Ten million? Go away, snakes!"

Triangle could not hiss anymore.
He was laughing too hard.

"Triangle!" said Square. "Is that you?"

"Yes!" said Triangle. "I know you are afraid of
snakes. I have played a sneaky trick on you!"

Square ran after Triangle, past small squares

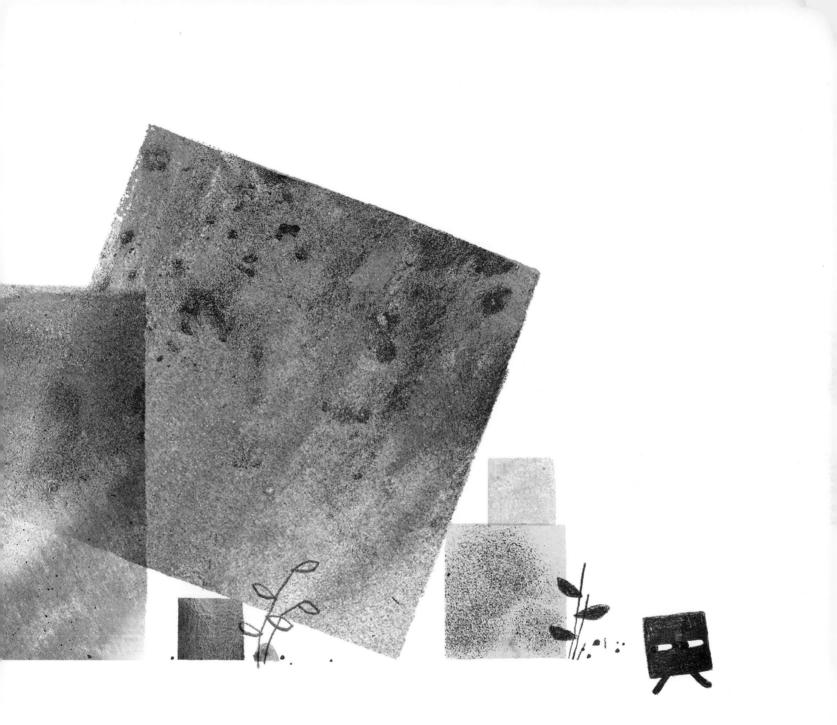

and medium squares and big squares.

He ran past the shapes

with no names,

past the big triangles

and medium triangles and small triangles,

up to Triangle's house and right through his door.

Almost.

"You are stuck!" Triangle laughed and laughed.

Then he stopped. His house was all dark.
Triangle was afraid of the dark.
"It's too dark!" said Triangle. "You're blocking
my light! Go away, you block! Leave my door!"

It was Square's turn to laugh.
"I know you are afraid of the dark. Now I have
played a sneaky trick on you! You see, Triangle,
this was my plan all along."

But do you really believe him?

To the Rexes: Adam, Marie, and Henry

M. B.

For Steve Malk

J. K.

MAC BARNETT & JON KLASSEN
have made three books together: *Sam and Dave Dig a Hole,*
which won a Caldecott Honor and an E. B. White Read
Aloud Award; *Extra Yarn,* which won a Caldecott Honor, an
E. B. White Read Aloud Award, and a *Boston Globe–Horn
Book* Award; and *Triangle,* which is the book you are
reading right now. They both live in California, but in
different cities. Jon's Canadian; Mac's not.